To Ethan—A. L.

For my first cousin Karla—F. C.

TREE OF HOPE

AMY LITTLESUGAR   FLOYD COOPER

PUFFIN BOOKS

Florrie's daddy and mama named her after the great actress Miss Florence Mills.

"My, but Miss Florence sparkled!" Daddy'd recall. For he was an actor himself in the old days, those golden days when the Lafayette Theatre up in Harlem was a glittering palace and the ladies in their cutaway shoes and the men in their silk toppers came to catch a show. Catch a star like Miss Florence Mills.

Daddy met Mama at the Lafayette. He'd landed a bit part in a new play. Every night he'd get the chance to stand on that big stage and face the lights.

"Encore! Encore!" the audience'd shout at the end.

Then one night, a pretty young woman handed him up a red, red rose.

"That was your mama," Daddy'd tell Florrie. "She was behind me being an actor in those days."

But then the Depression hit. Newspapers shouted "HARD TIMES!" and folks, especially in Harlem, weren't thinking about going to plays. Men and women in threadbare coats stood in long lines—twice as long as anyplace else—just for a free potato. They were hungry. Hungry for food and jobs—not theater!

Florrie's Mama found cleaning work at the beauty shop. Daddy left the stage. No one needed actors now. Not black actors. That was certain. So he put on an apron and got himself another job—frying donuts at the Allnight Bakery.

And the Lafayette Theatre became a big ghostly place filled with rats and spiders till only one thing remained of those old days, those golden days. One twisted and crooked thing.

It was a tree.

A tree that grew right beside the Lafayette. And because it did, when most everything in Harlem seemed to have died, theater people gave it a special name, Tree of Hope.

"Is it a magic tree, Daddy?" Florrie asked one evening.

"Yeah, Sugar," Daddy nodded. For it was said that one wish on it would bring you good luck—even in those hard times.

Daddy reached out his hand to the tree like it was an old friend. He told it how much he missed being an actor. How he missed standing on a big stage, facing the lights.

"Florrie," Daddy said, "I'd give up this here apron in a second for another chance."

"Been wishin' on that tree again, huh?" Mama scolded when they got home late.

"I never seen such daydreamers. We ain't got but two dimes to rub together, and you all go wishin' on some fool tree!"

Florrie stared out the alley window late that night. Empty buildings boarded up tight stared back. Once, folks lived in those buildings. Before the hard times. Now the peddlers' wagons were filled with their belongings.

"Chairs! Chairs to sell!" they'd cry through the Harlem streets.

Florrie closed her eyes. "Please," she whispered, wondering if the tree might hear, "please, let my daddy be an actor again."

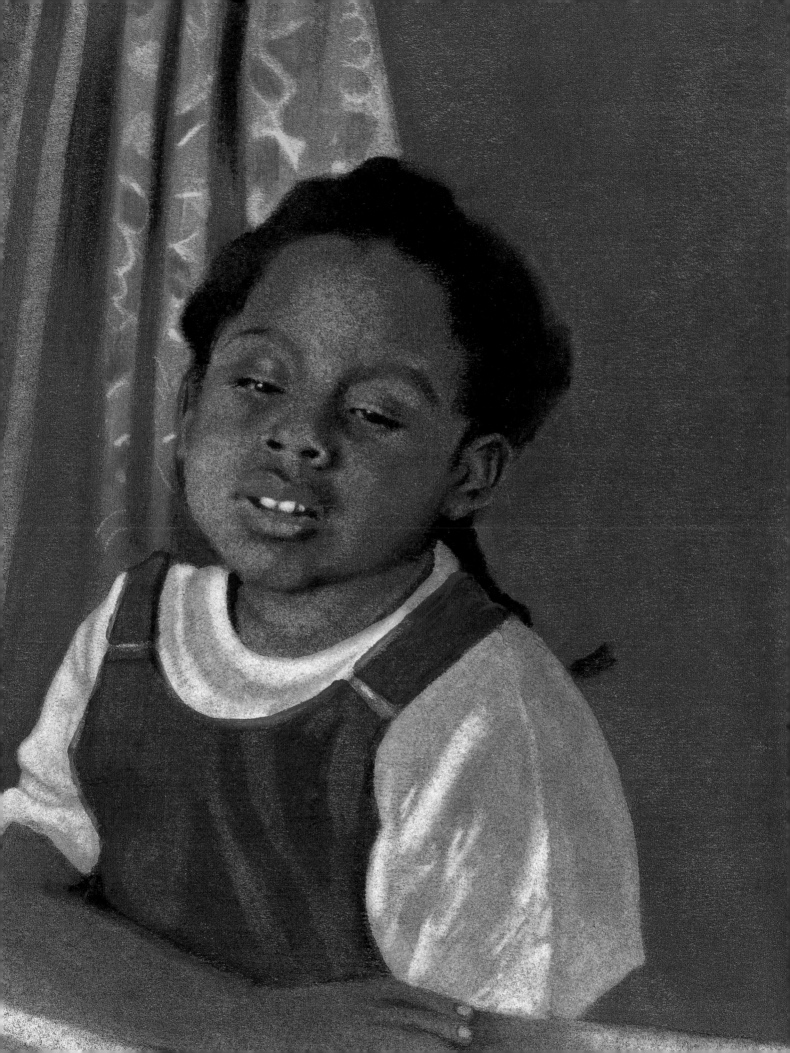

But no matter how much she wished, Daddy still came dragging home each night from the Allnight Bakery. And the Lafayette Theatre stayed closed.

"Mama gave up dreamin' long ago," Daddy told Florrie. "But don't you never."

So Florrie wished even harder. And one night, looking up into a sky full of stars, she imagined her wish. Like a leaf. Twirling and fluttering past those peddlers' wagons and empty buildings. All the way up Seventh Avenue—to the Tree of Hope.

"Please," Florrie cried out loud this time, "please, let my daddy be an actor again!"

And the very next day it happened. By order of President Roosevelt himself. The old Lafayette Theatre was opening its doors once more.

Up and down the Harlem streets, the news spread fast. Dancers, singers, stage hands, and actors—they'd all be needed. They'd all get a chance again.

Daddy laughed. Then he cried.

It seemed Florrie's wish'd come true.

Tryouts, they learned, would be at the Elks' Hall. First for some plays by black writers like Countee Cullen and Zora Neale Hurston. And then for William Shakespeare's *Macbeth*!

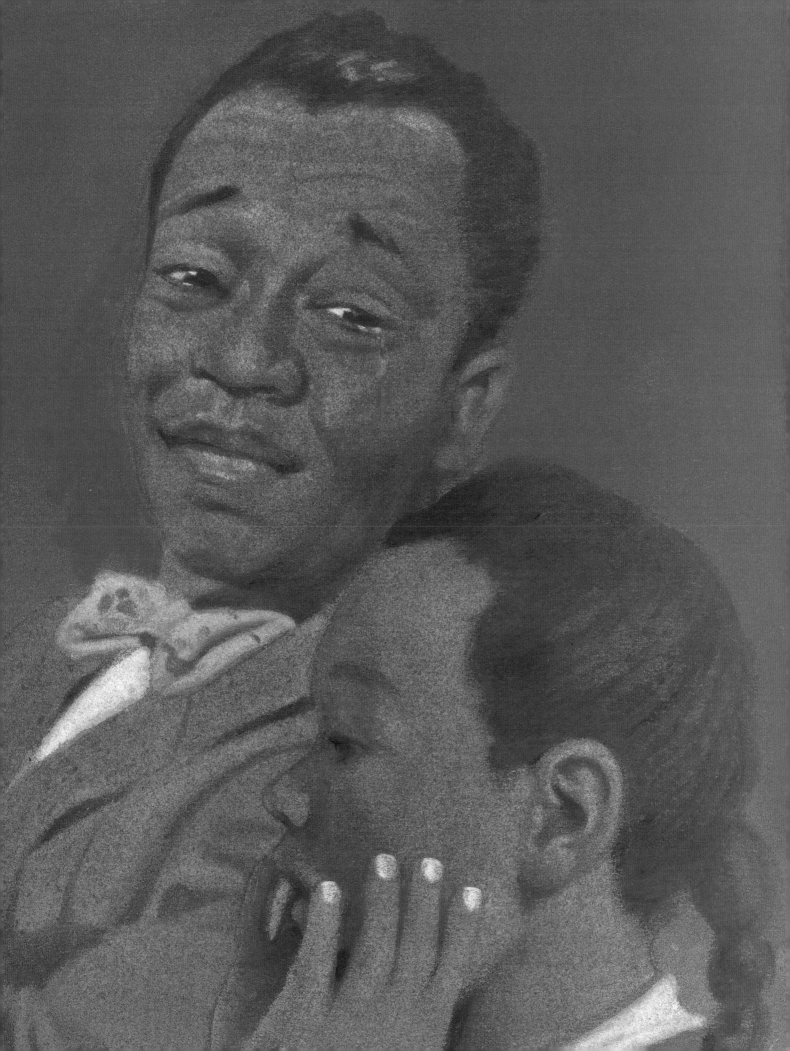

Daddy felt let down. He'd wanted to be in a play by a black playwright. Those plays were filled. But he went and tried out anyway, for *Macbeth*.

"Come on, Sugar," he said, and took Florrie along.

The place was filled with hopefuls.

"Next!" roared a voice deep as thunder.

Florrie's mouth hung open. It was a white man! He had black eyes and wild black hair, and a rumpled shirt. Someone said he was the director, "Mr. Welles."

"Next," Mr. Welles growled. "NEXT!"

Florrie's heart skipped a beat. It was Daddy's turn.

Daddy'd never read much Shakespeare. But he liked this story about an evil king from long ago Scotland. So when he read the only line he was told to say, he stood straight. His voice reached clear across the room . . .

"Ay, my lord. It shall be done!"

Mr. Welles scribbled fast. "We'll call you," he told Daddy.

Weeks passed. Nerve-jangling weeks. Daddy went to work at the Allnight Bakery. Only his heart wasn't there. Not frying donuts over a hot griddle anymore. He was on a big stage now. Facing the lights.

Then the news came.

"I'm to play a soldier!" Daddy told Mama, swinging her around and around.

Florrie jumped so high, she felt she had wings on.

But some folks in Harlem were angry.

"Shakespeare's a white man," they argued. "We oughta only be doin' plays written 'bout us. Them people at the Lafayette've come to Harlem just to laugh at us!"

Daddy'd get quiet when he heard such talk.

"There will be plays written about us," he'd say. "This is Harlem's *Macbeth*—you'll see."

But even Daddy was surprised at what happened next.

Macbeth was about a greedy nobleman and his greedy wife who'd stop at nothing to become king and queen—even murdering their good king Duncan. The story always took place on the Scottish heath. But not this time, Mr. Welles decided. This *Macbeth* would take place on the island of Haiti, where the terrible king Christophe once ruled.

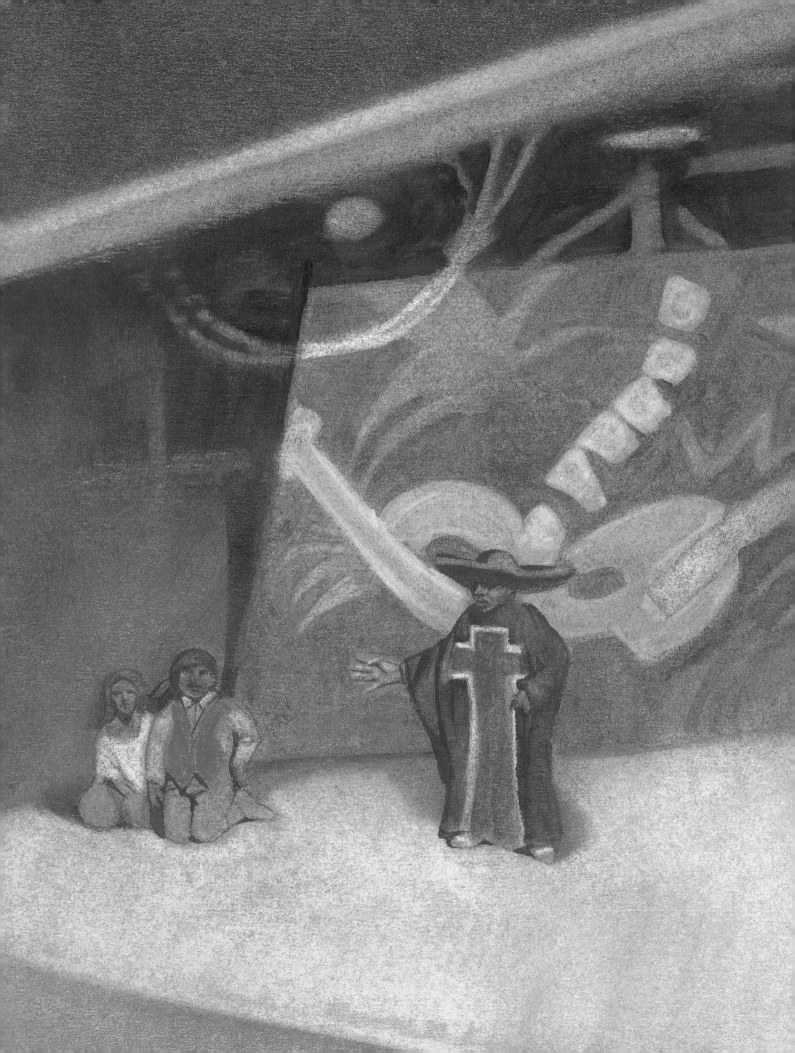

Almost all of Harlem was behind Mr. Welles now. Those
from Haiti. The West Indies. The Caribbean. Florrie heard it
on street corners and stoops.

"C'est ça." They nodded. "Okay!" For, now, it really was
Harlem's *Macbeth*!

Black stage hands could hardly wait to get to work. And
Florrie got to go backstage to watch. Soon they'd created a
monstrous castle surrounded by a dark green jungle.

Three "conjure men" from the west of Africa were even hired. On drums made from the skin of goats, they'd tell Macbeth's terrible fortune—some nights, Florrie imagined, waking all of Harlem.

A drum, a drum! Macbeth doth come.
Shamkoko, Shanwable, O beri-beri!

From midnight on, every night, all that long cold winter, they'd rehearse their parts. Some, like the actress who played the wicked Lady Macbeth, already knew her lines. "Here's the smell of blood still . . . Oh! Oh! Oh!"

But others held things up, missing words here and there. "Get that scene right!" Mr. Welles'd roar.

Daddy'd come home bone tired, for he'd kept his job at the Allnight Bakery. Mama didn't like it, but Daddy said that's how it was in the old days. The golden days.

"Don't you remember?" he'd ask Mama gently. Only Mama'd turn away.

Finally, after months of hard work, it was opening night. Up and down the Harlem streets, shimmering signs made a bright red promise: *MACBETH* BY WILLIAM SHAKESPEARE.

Earlier, Daddy'd walked Florrie up to see the Tree of Hope.

"Close your eyes, Sugar," he said. "That's it! Now open 'em."

The tree, dressed in ribbons and a rainbow of balloons, was beautiful!

"We did it late last night," Daddy explained, reaching in his pocket. "Here, this one's for you."

Florrie held the long pink ribbon. She wished she could hold on to everything this way. Harlem. Daddy. Even tonight.

Then Daddy lifted Florrie up. She tied her ribbon around the longest branch on the tree. "Watch for me tonight," he whispered. "Near the end. And tell Mama to have you here by six. I'll get the box-office man to let you help out!"

Harlem was a sea of people that night. Honking cars and snarling taxis jammed the streets, while a brass band played on and on. The Lafayette was a glittering palace, and Florrie was there. But not Mama. She had to work the late shift at the beauty shop. She really had given up dreaming, Florrie thought.

"Playbills!" she called, her small stack going fast. She kept looking for Mama. Hoping she'd come. Yet each face that passed through those lobby doors was the wrong one.

Soon the doors were closing. With only one playbill left, she started to put it in her pocket, when she heard someone ask, "May I have that, please?"

Florrie looked up. "Mama!"

Mama smiled. Two forty-cent tickets in her hand.

"Come on, girl," she said. "Let's go!"

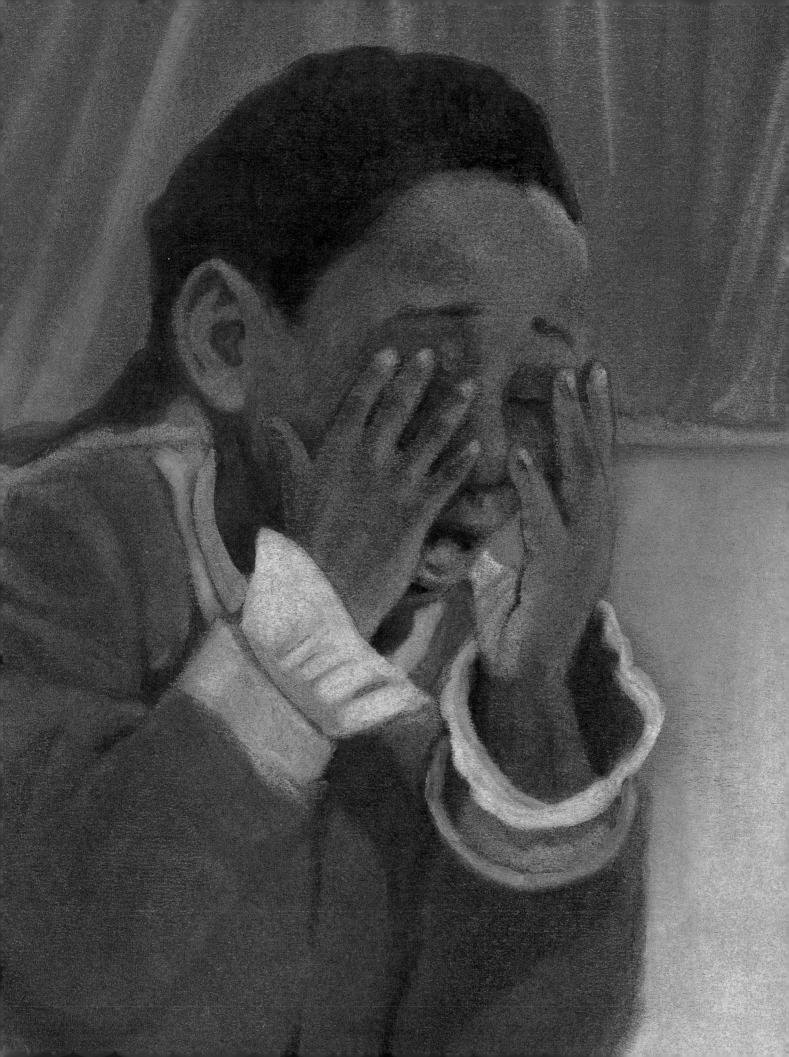

The curtain went up at half past nine on a monstrous
castle and a dark green jungle and the conjure men—
their gold and diamond teeth glimmering in the darkness.
They'd put a spell on Macbeth. An evil spell.

A drum, a drum! Macbeth doth come.
Shamkoko, Shanwable, O beri-beri!

Florrie shivered and sat close to Mama. She didn't like it
when the kettledrums rumbled and the cymbals crashed.
And she hid her face when Macbeth and Lady Macbeth
killed the good king Duncan.

But then it was the scene where Macbeth was crowned
king. The stage was bathed in silver light, and music played
as ladies in silk dresses and gentlemen in pink and green
and blue and orange danced and twirled. Florried smiled.
It was perfect this time!

But where was Daddy? she wondered. The play was
almost over.

"Hush," said Mama, her eyes shining. "Look!"

And there he stood near the castle gate, in a satin uniform and shiny black boots. Then he spoke the line Florrie and Mama knew by heart.

"Ay, my lord. It shall be done!"

Florrie got so excited she nearly forgot the sword fight scene. Thwack! Twang! Woosh! Zinggg!!

High up on the castle's ramparts stood the villain Macbeth. The hero, Macduff, raised his pistol. Florrie gasped, and there was a bloodcurdling scream as Macbeth fell to his death!

"The charm's wound up!" the conjure men cried. It was over.

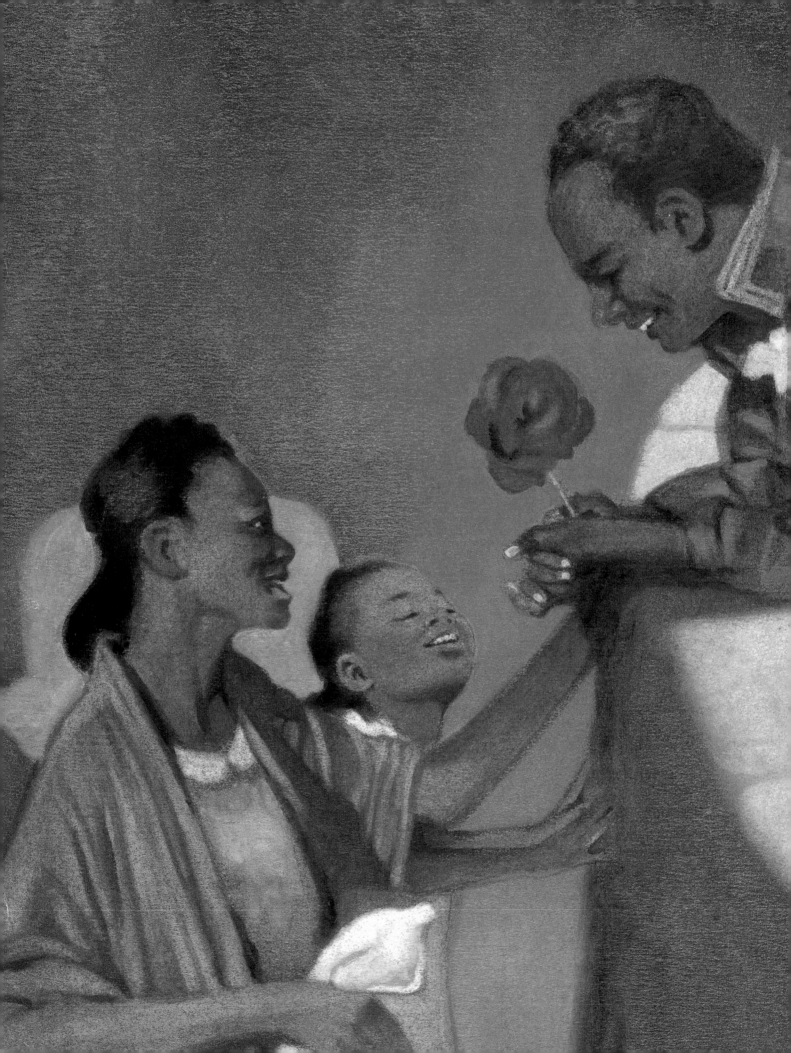

And the audience was on its feet, cheering, clapping.
"Encore! Encore!"
Suddenly, Mama grabbed Florrie's hand, and before she knew it, they were headed for the stage.

The entire cast was there. Even Mr. Welles. They waved to the crowd and took their bows under a shower of bouquets. Only Mama wasn't looking at them. She was looking at Daddy. Standing on that big stage. Facing the lights.

Daddy saw Mama, too. He smiled the biggest smile Florrie'd ever seen, and came and kneeled down.

And right there, Mama did something Florrie'd never forget. She reached inside her coat and took out a rose. A red, red rose. Then, just like in the old days, the golden days, she smiled back at Daddy and handed him up Florrie's wish.

Author's Note

African-American actors had been starring in Shakesperean productions for more than a hundred years. So in 1935, when Orson Welles chose to stage Harlem's version of *Macbeth*, or 'voodoo *Macbeth*' as it was also called, an all-black cast rose to the challenge.

Why? Maybe because even though these were the darkest days of the Great Depression, people in Harlem had not forgotten the 'golden days' of what was known in the 1920's as the Harlem Renaissance. For the first time, black writers, poets and artists like Langston Hughes, Countee Cullen and Aaron Douglas had begun to tap into their own culture; producing, through their art, a brand new American viewpoint.

Now in the thirties, Harlem's *Macbeth* would, in a way, achieve that too, proving that black actors could tackle those stage roles once reserved only for whites. Even after the Federal Theater Project (which had funded dramas like *Macbeth*) ended, black theater wouldn't die. And in 1940, the American Negro Theater would be born.

As black critic Errol Aubrey Jones would proudly write the morning after Harlem *Macbeth*'s smash opening night:

"The theater lives again. Hurrah!"

Patricia Lee Gauch, Editor

PUFFIN BOOKS
Published by the Penguin Group
Penguin Putnam Books for Young Readers, 345 Hudson Street,
New York, New York 10014, U.S.A.
Penguin Books Ltd, 27 Wrights Lane, London W8 5TZ, England
Penguin Books Australia Ltd, Ringwood, Victoria, Australia
Penguin Books Canada Ltd, 10 Alcorn Avenue, Toronto, Ontario, Canada M4V 3B2
Penguin Books (N.Z.) Ltd, 182–190 Wairau Road, Auckland 10, New Zealand
Penguin Books Ltd, Registered Offices: Harmondsworth, Middlesex, England

First published in the United States of America by Philomel Books,
a division of Penguin Putnam Books for Young Readers, 1999
Published by Puffin Books, a division of Penguin Putnam Books for Young
Readers, 2001

10 9 8 7 6 5 4 3 2 1

Text copyright © Amy Littlesugar, 1999. Illustrations copyright © Floyd Cooper,
1999. All rights reserved

THE LIBRARY OF CONGRESS HAS CATALOGED THE PHILOMEL EDITION AS FOLLOWS:
Littlesugar, Amy. Tree of Hope / written by Amy Littlesugar;
illustrated by Floyd Cooper.   p.   cm.   Summary: Florrie's daddy used to be a
stage actor in Harlem before the Depression forced the Lafayette Theatre to close,
but he gets a chance to act again when Orson Welles reopens the theater to stage
an all-black version of Macbeth. 1. Afro-Americans—Juvenile fiction. [1. Afro-
Americans—Fiction. 2. Actors and actresses—Fiction. 3. Depressions—1929—
Fiction. 4. Harlem (New York, N.Y.)—Fiction] I. Cooper, Floyd, ill. II. Title.
PZ7 .L7362Tr 1999 [E]—dc21 98-12853 CIP AC ISBN 0-399-23300-8

Puffin Books ISBN 0-698-11903-7

Printed in the United States of America

Bibliography

Anderson, Jervis. This Was Harlem. New York: Farrar, Straus & Giroux, 1982.

Andrews, Bert. In the Shadow of the Great White Way: Images from the Black Theater. New York: Thunder's Mouth Press, 1989.

Bogle, Donald. Brown Sugar. New York: Harmony Books, 1980.

Callow, Simon. Orson Wells: The Road to Xanadu. New York: Viking, 1995.

Halliburton, Warren J., with Ernest Kaiser. Harlem: A History of Broken Dreams. New York: Zenith Books, 1974.

Hausman, John. Run – Through. New York: Simon & Schuster, 1972.

Huberman, Caryn, and JoAnne Wetzel. Onstage/Backstage. Minneapolis: Carolrhoda Books, Inc., 1987.

Lamb, Charles and Mary. Romeo and Juliet. London and New York: Franklin Watts Ltd., 1971.

Ross, Stewart. Shakespeare and Macbeth: The Story Behind The Play. New York: Penguin Group, 1994.

Siskind, Aaron. Harlem Documents: Photographs 1932–1940. Providence: Matrix Publications, Inc., 1981.

Smith, Wendy. "The Play That Electrified Harlem," Civilization: The Magazine of the Library of Congress, Jan. - Feb. 1996.

Willis - Brainwaite, Deborah. VanDerZee: Photographer 1886–1983. New York: Harry Abrams, Inc., 1993.